HORSE — 30 MILES (48 KM) PER HOUR

SKATEBOARD — 15 MILES (24 KM) PER HOUR

DOG — 20 MILES (32 KM) PER HOUR

NASA X-43A — Mach 9.6 (approx. 7,000 MILES PER HOUR)   NOW THAT'S FAST!: NASA X-43A

JACKRABBIT — 45 MILES (72 KM) PER HOUR

HUMAN — 12 MILES (19 KM) PER HOUR

BICYCLE — 15 MILES (24 KM) PER HOUR

This book was donated by
United Library Services
Calgary, Alberta

NOW THAT'S FAST!
NASA X-43A

KATE RIGGS

CREATIVE EDUCATION • CREATIVE PAPERBACKS

Published by Creative Education and
Creative Paperbacks
P.O. Box 227, Mankato, Minnesota 56002
Creative Education and Creative Paperbacks
are imprints of The Creative Company
www.thecreativecompany.us

Design by Blue Design;
production by Dana Cheit
Art direction by Rita Marshall
Printed in the United States of America

Photographs by Alamy (NASA Image
Collection, RGB Ventures/SuperStock),
NASA (Tony Landis, NASA, Jim Ross, Carla
Thomas, Tom Tschida, Brent Wood)

Copyright © 2019 Creative Education,
Creative Paperbacks
International copyright reserved in all
countries. No part of this book may be
reproduced in any form without written
permission from the publisher.

Library of Congress Cataloging-in-
Publication Data
Names: Riggs, Kate, author.
Title: NASA X-43A / Kate Riggs.
Series: Now that's fast!
Includes bibliographical references and
index.
Summary: A fast-paced, high-interest
overview of the features, purpose, history,
and high-speed capabilities of NASA's
X-43A—the fastest unmanned aircraft in
the world.
Identifiers: ISBN 978-1-64026-032-0
(hardcover) / ISBN 978-1-62832-587-4 (pbk)
/ ISBN 978-1-64000-061-2 (eBook)
This title has been submitted for CIP
processing under LCCN 2018944094.

CCSS: RI.1.1, 2, 4, 5, 6, 7; RI.2.2, 5, 6, 7, 10;
RI.3.1, 5, 7, 8; RF.1.1, 3, 4; RF.2.3, 4

First Edition HC 9 8 7 6 5 4 3 2 1
First Edition PBK 9 8 7 6 5 4 3 2 1

Table of Contents

Hypersonic Aircraft	6
Rocket Booster	10
Ground Control	13
Testing the X-43A	14
Future Flight	18
Zooming through the Air	20
Breaking Down the X-43A	22
Fast Facts	23
Glossary	24
Read More	24
Index	24

HYPERSONIC AIRCRAFT

Aircraft are fast vehicles. Those that fly faster than five times the speed of sound are **hypersonic**. They can be powered by scramjets. These are jet **engines** that "breathe" air.

Super-fast aircraft measure speed using **Mach numbers**. Mach 1 is the speed of sound. Mach 2 is twice the speed of sound. X-43A was so fast that it went almost 10 times the speed of sound!

ROCKET BOOSTER

X-43A did not have wings. It was about 12 feet (3.7 m) long. It weighed 3,000 pounds (1,361 kg). A rocket carried X-43A to boost its height and speed at first. X-43A fit onto the nose of the rocket.

GROUND CONTROL

No one sat inside the X-43A. People controlled it from the ground. Each X-43A crashed into the Pacific Ocean at the end of its flight.

TESTING THE X-43A

NASA built three X-43As. Each was used for a different test. It took almost eight years to get the models just right. But the first flight in 2001 failed! The rocket carrying X-43A went off course. The controllers had to destroy it before it crashed and hurt anyone.

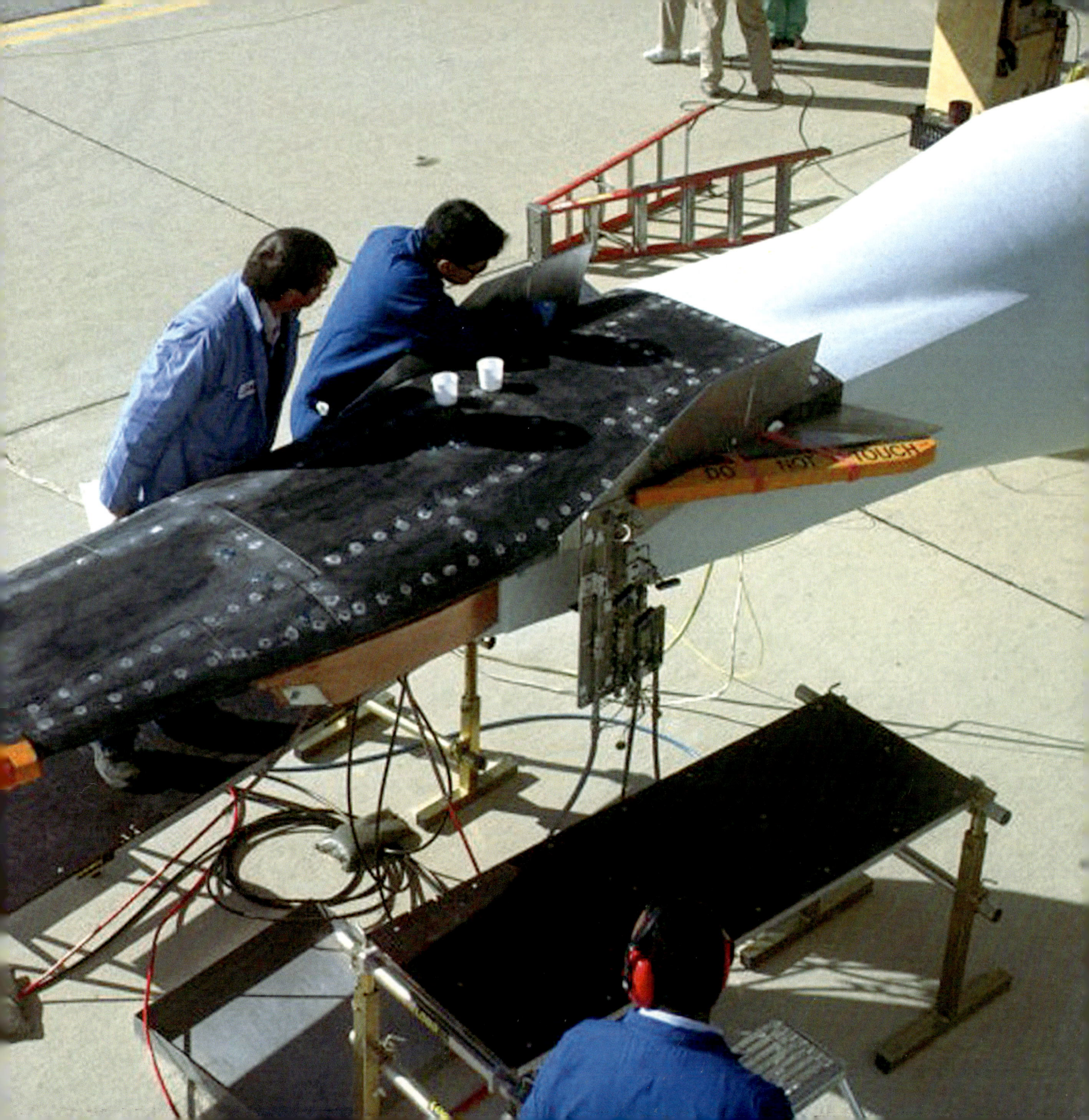

The second test was in March 2004 (pictured). This time, the X-43A set a jet-powered record for speed. A few months later, the third test broke that record! It reached Mach 9.6.

FUTURE FLIGHT

The X-43As helped NASA learn more about hypersonic flight. Other air and space vehicles might fly as fast as X-43A someday. They could be even faster!

The third X-43A flew on its scramjet for only 10 seconds. Jet engines that last longer could go farther.

ZOOMING THROUGH THE AIR

Planes take off. Rockets launch. Jet engines burn as aircraft zoom through the air. New tests uncover more facts about flight!

BREAKING DOWN THE X-43A

fin

aftbody

LENGTH: 12 FEET (3.7 M) LONG

WIDTH: 5 FEET (1.5 M) WIDE